SCOOBY-DOO!™
and the
WITCHING HOUR

DEVELOPING READER · LEVEL 2 · 250-750 WORDS

By Sonia Sander
Illustrated by Duendes del Sur

SCHOLASTIC INC.
New York Toronto London Auckland Sydney
Mexico City New Delhi Hong Kong Buenos Aires

ISBN-13: 978-0-545-16106-0
ISBN-10: 0-545-16106-1

Designed by Michael Massen

12 11 10 9 8 7 6 5 4 3 2 1   9 10 11 12 13/0

Printed in the U.S.A.
First printing, July 2009

It was Halloween. Scooby and Shaggy were picking out a pumpkin.

"Like, look at all of the pumpkins, Scoob! *Mm-mm-mm!* That sure is a lot of pumpkin pies. I'll race you to the biggest one!" said Shaggy.

Shaggy looked all over the pumpkin patch. "Roo!" cried Scooby, trying to scare Shaggy. Shaggy was scared, all right, but not by Scooby.

It was a mean, green witch that scared Shaggy.
"Zoinks! Like, let's make some tracks — and
fast!" cried Shaggy.
The witch chased them out of the patch.

"Check this out, gang," called Fred. "Wendy Waters is opening a water park."

"Jeepers," said Daphne. "There's no room in town for a Whirly World."

"That has not stopped her," said Velma. "She wants the whole town to sell her some land."

All of a sudden, Shaggy and Scooby almost ran the gang down.

"Whoa there!" said Fred. "Where's the fire?"

"Boy, am I glad to see you guys and get away from that creepy witch!" cried Shaggy.

It was time for the Halloween party at the pumpkin patch.

"Like, no way am I going back to that creepy place," said Shaggy.

"That's too bad," said Fred. "You will miss all the good food."

Shaggy and Scooby didn't need to hear any more.

"Rood?" said Scooby.

"Like, we're there!" cried Shaggy.

Scooby and Shaggy joined the gang for the big party.

But they were still worried.

"Like, I sure hope that weirdo witch doesn't show up," said Shaggy.

Scooby and Shaggy didn't waste any time finding the food.

But they didn't just find the food.
They found the witch, too!
"Ah-ah-ah-ah-ah!" cried the witch.

"Relp! Relp!" cried Scooby.
"Zoinks! The creepy witch is back!" cried
Shaggy.
"That old story again?" asked Velma.

"It's true! It's true! We have seen her, too!"
cried a group of kids.

"Sounds like we have a mystery on our
hands, gang," said Fred.

"Ruh-roh!" said Scooby.
"Like, I'm with you pal," added Shaggy.
"We're out of here."

"Will you stay for a Scooby Snack?" asked Daphne.
Scooby couldn't say no to a Scooby Snack. He and Shaggy agreed to stay and help.

Fred, Daphne, and Velma headed to the
barn. They wanted to check the last place the
witch had been.

Daphne tripped on a loose board. "Jeepers!"
she cried.

The witch's voice rang out again. "Ah-ah-ah-ah-ah!"

"It looks like stepping on this board starts a recording," said Velma.

Fred, Daphne, and Velma found one more clue inside the barn.

"Now we know how the witch flies through the air," said Velma.

24

"It's all thanks to a slide show," added Daphne.

"I think it's time to find out who's dressing up like a witch," said Fred.

Shaggy and Scooby had already found the witch. They tried to run away, but they didn't get very far. Shaggy's bandages got stuck on a nail.

Now Shaggy and Scooby could only run in circles.

The more they ran, the more the bandages unrolled.

Luckily, the bandages wound around the witch. Soon the witch was all tied up!

"There's only one person who wants land bad enough to scare folks," said Velma.

"If it weren't for you meddling kids," said Wendy Waters, "I would have gotten my land and my Whirly World!"

With the witch mystery solved, it was time to have fun.

"Rummy!" Scooby said, licking his chops.

"Like, you said it, Scoob!" said Shaggy.

They shared a giant pile of treats.

"Happy Halloween!"